Captain America: Meet Sam Wilson!

Senior Editor David Fentiman
Project Art Editor Chris Gould
Senior Production Editor Jennifer Murray
Senior Production Controller Mary Slater
Managing Editor Rachel Lawrence
Managing Art Editor Vicky Short
Publishing Director Mark Searle

Designed by Ray Bryant
Reading Consultant Barbara Marinak

First American Edition, 2024
Published in the United States by DK Publishing
1745 Broadway, 20th Floor, New York, NY 10019

DK, a Division of Penguin Random House LLC
24 25 26 27 28 10 9 8 7 6 5 4 3 2 1
001–338689–Apr/24

© 2024 MARVEL

All rights reserved.
Without limiting the rights under the copyright reserved above, no part of this publication may be reproduced, stored in or introduced into a retrieval system, or transmitted, in any form, or by any means (electronic, mechanical, photocopying, recording, or otherwise), without the prior written permission of the copyright owner.
Published in Great Britain by Dorling Kindersley Limited

A catalog record for this book
is available from the Library of Congress.
ISBN 978-0-7440-9224-0 (Paperback)
ISBN 978-0-7440-9225-7 (Hardcover)

DK books are available at special discounts when purchased in bulk
for sales promotions, premiums, fund-raising, or educational use.
For details, contact: DK Publishing Special Markets,
1745 Broadway, 20th Floor, New York, NY 10019
SpecialSales@dk.com

Printed and bound in China

www.dk.com
www.marvel.com

 This book was made with Forest Stewardship Council™ certified paper—one small step in DK's commitment to a sustainable future. Learn more at
www.dk.com/uk/information/sustainability

Level 3

Captain America: Meet Sam Wilson!

By Mayonn Paasewe-Valchev

Contents

6	Meet Sam Wilson!
8	Captain Gear
10	The First Captain America
12	Sam Meets Steve Rogers
14	The Falcon
16	A New Captain
18	Growing up in Harlem
20	Hard Times
22	Doing the Right Thing
24	The Avengers
26	Bird Powers
28	Redwing
30	Battle Skills
32	Sam Wilson in Action
34	Mighty Captains
36	People Problems

38 Sam's Friends
40 Enemies
42 Sam Saves the Day
44 Soaring
46 Glossary
47 Index
48 Quiz

Meet Sam Wilson!

Sam Wilson soars across the city with jet-powered wings. As Captain America, he fights to keep the world safe and fair. Sam likes helping people. He likes birds, too.

Captain Gear

Sam wears his Captain America gear when he goes on a mission.

Shield
Captain America's shield is made of a powerful metal called vibranium. It is almost indestructible.

Jet-powered Wings
Sam's jet-powered wings allow him to fly at high speeds. They can fold up when he is on the ground.

Goggles
Goggles protect Cap's eyes when he is flying fast through the air.

Super Hero Suit
Gloves provide a good grip when Cap throws his shield. Knee pads prevent Cap's knees from getting hurt.

The First Captain America

There has been more than one hero called Captain America. Steve Rogers was the first. He is strong and brave. Sometimes, Steve shares his Captain America duty with others. He can count on friends like Sam Wilson to step in and help.

Sam Meets Steve Rogers

Sam and Steve met while trapped on an island with criminals. Being on the island was not safe. But Steve had an idea. He trained Sam to be a strong fighter. Together they teamed up and defeated the bad guys. Steve and Sam have been best friends since.

The Falcon

Steve Rogers thought Sam would make a great hero. He inspired Sam to choose a Super Hero name, suit, and mask. Sam became the flying hero called Falcon! Sam was known as the Falcon before he became Captain America.

A New Captain

During a battle with a dangerous villain, Steve Rogers lost all of his super-powers and was turned into an old man. Without his strength, Steve could no longer carry his shield. He asked Sam to take over as Captain America. Sam stepped in to help his friend. After Steve recovered, they both shared being Captain America.

Growing up in Harlem

Sam grew up in Harlem, New York. His father was a pastor. On Sundays, Sam attended church with his brother Gideon and sister Sarah. He also trained pigeons. Sam owned the largest pigeon coop in his city.

Hard Times

Sam's parents were killed by criminals when he was still young. Growing up without a father and mother was hard for Sam. He tried his best to be a strong big brother. Sam looked after his brother and sister and kept them safe.

Family Comes First
Now they are all grown up, Sam is still very close to his sister. He is a caring uncle to her children.

Doing the Right Thing

Sam knew his parents wanted him to make good decisions, even if they were no longer around. Sam helped people in his community. Sometimes he served food to people who had no homes. He also went to college. Sam worked hard to do the right thing.

The Avengers

As Captain America, Sam led a team of mighty Super Heroes known as the Avengers. He joined missions with champions like Iron Man and Spider-Man. As a member of the Avengers, Sam saved the world from dangerous villains and aliens. Sam showed his team that he could be a good leader.

Bird Powers

Sam has a special friendship with birds! Look at how he uses his bird powers.

Bird Mind Reading
Sam shares a telepathic bond with birds. If they sense danger, so will Sam.

Bird Allies
Sam's bird friends will join him to battle his enemies.

Bird Vision
Sam can see what birds see, even villains hiding in caves or behind bushes.

27

Redwing

Squawk! Sam has a pet falcon named Redwing. Sam and Redwing are a great team. When they are on a mission together, Redwing flies ahead to scout the area. He will warn Sam if danger lurks. Redwing is a good spy for Sam.

Battle Skills

Sam is a trained martial artist. He uses karate skills to defeat his enemies. Sam has also had gymnastics training. He twists, bends, and does backflips during combat. He can throw his shield far and fast, and hit moving targets with it.

Sam Wilson in Action

Sam often goes on missions to fight a criminal group known as Hydra. Hydra want to take over the world. Sam won't let them. He swoops upon them and spoils their plans. Sam is brave and will always fight to protect other people.

Mighty Captains

Sometimes Sam Wilson and Steve Rogers team up to fight their enemies. They go on missions together and wield their Captain America shields. As good friends, they help and defend each other against super villains and criminals.

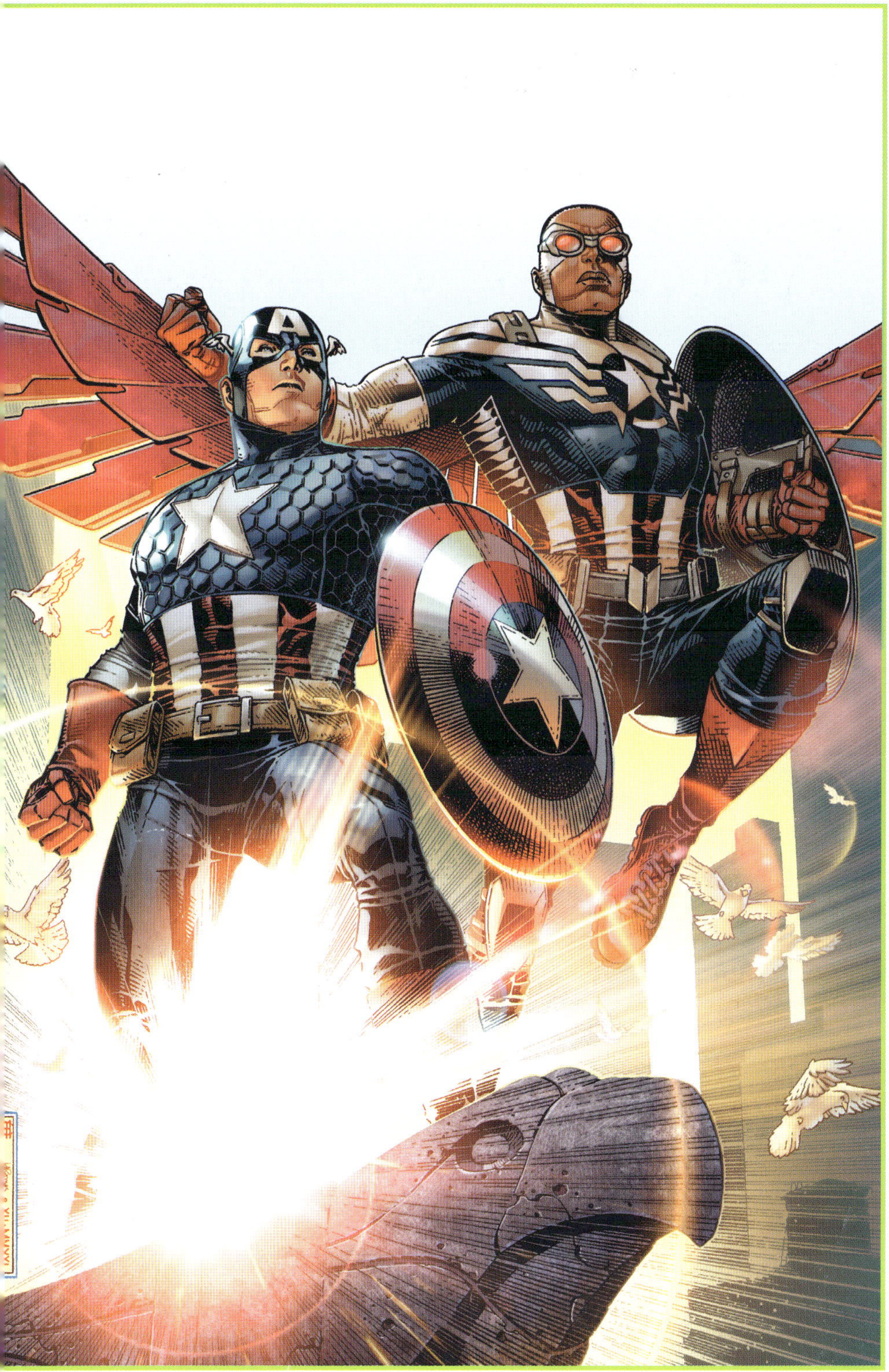

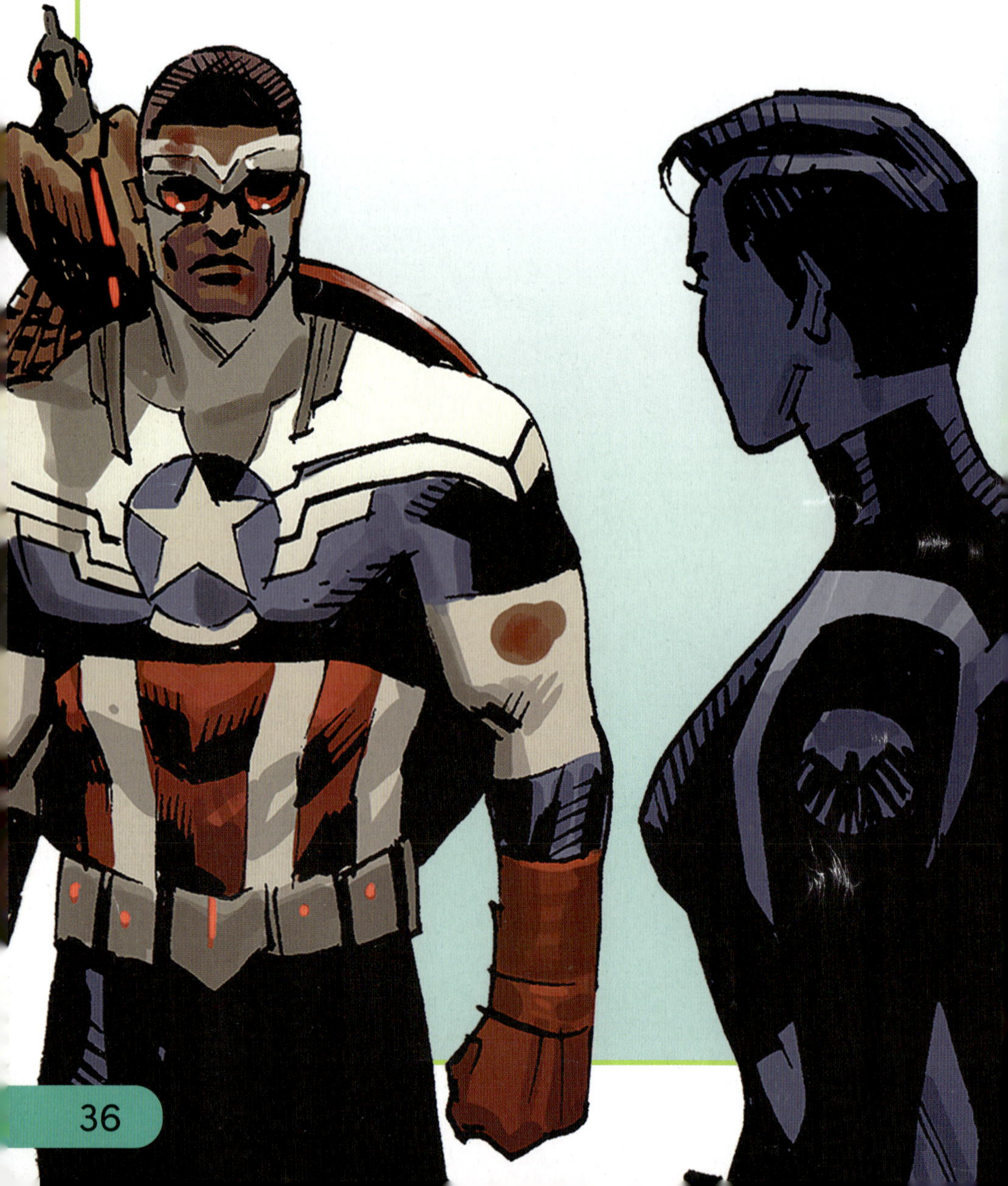

People Problems

Some people prefer the first Captain America instead of Sam Wilson. Others aren't always thankful for the work Sam does. Sometimes this makes Sam unhappy. Still, he keeps being a good Super Hero, even when the job is hard.

Sam's Friends

Even Super Heroes need help from friends. Misty Knight is one of Sam's good pals. She was once a police officer. Misty lost one of her arms and now has a robotic arm instead. She helps Sam defeat villains, even a band of mean monsters on a snowy mountain.

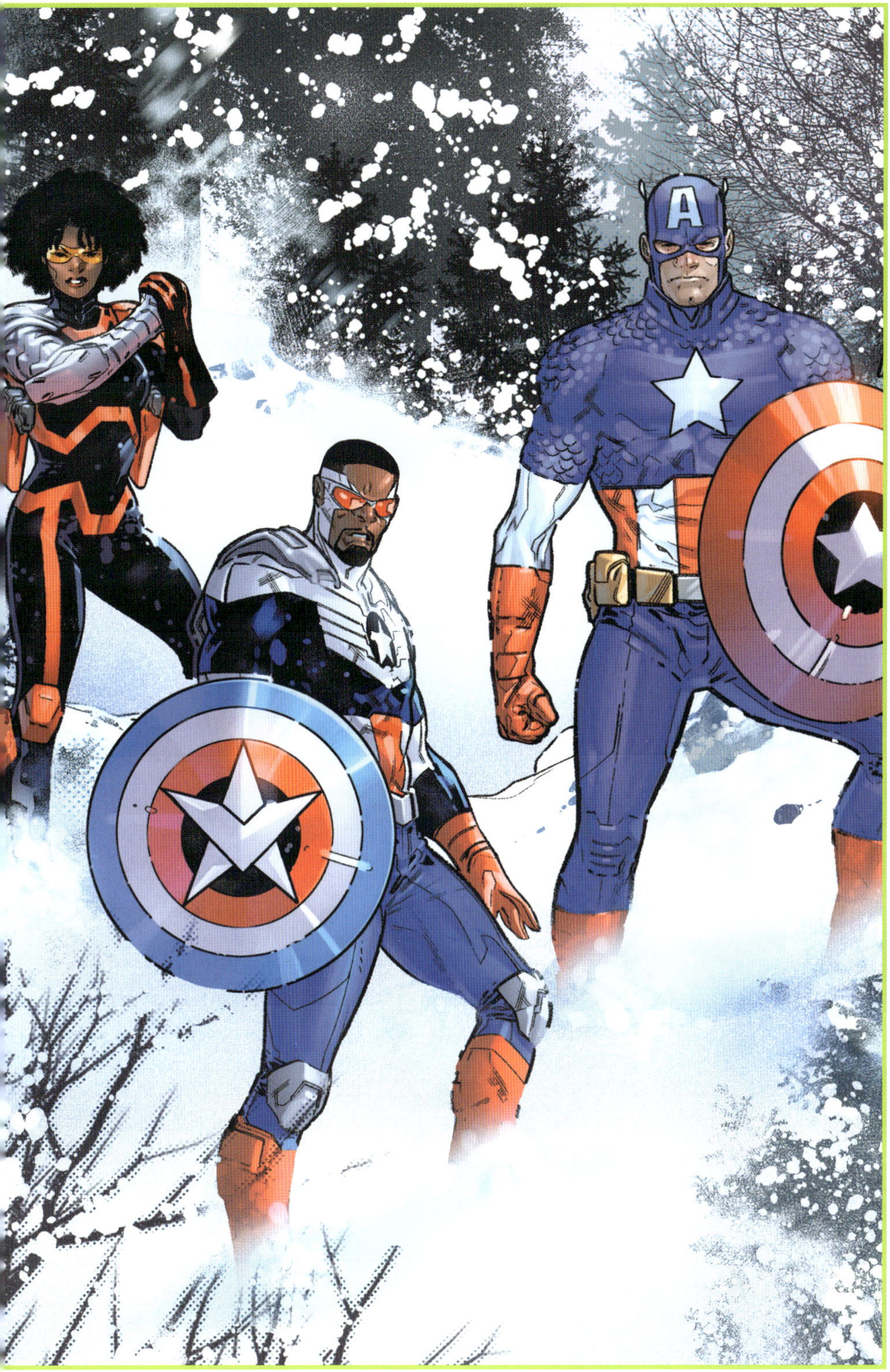

Enemies

Sam has many enemies. One of them is a sneaky villain named Red Skull. Red Skull plays dangerous mind tricks using a powerful Cosmic Cube. In fact, he once brainwashed Sam. Luckily, Sam is now able to escape Red Skull's mind control traps.

Flying Protector
Sam's wings allow him to rescue people from places that other heroes cannot reach.

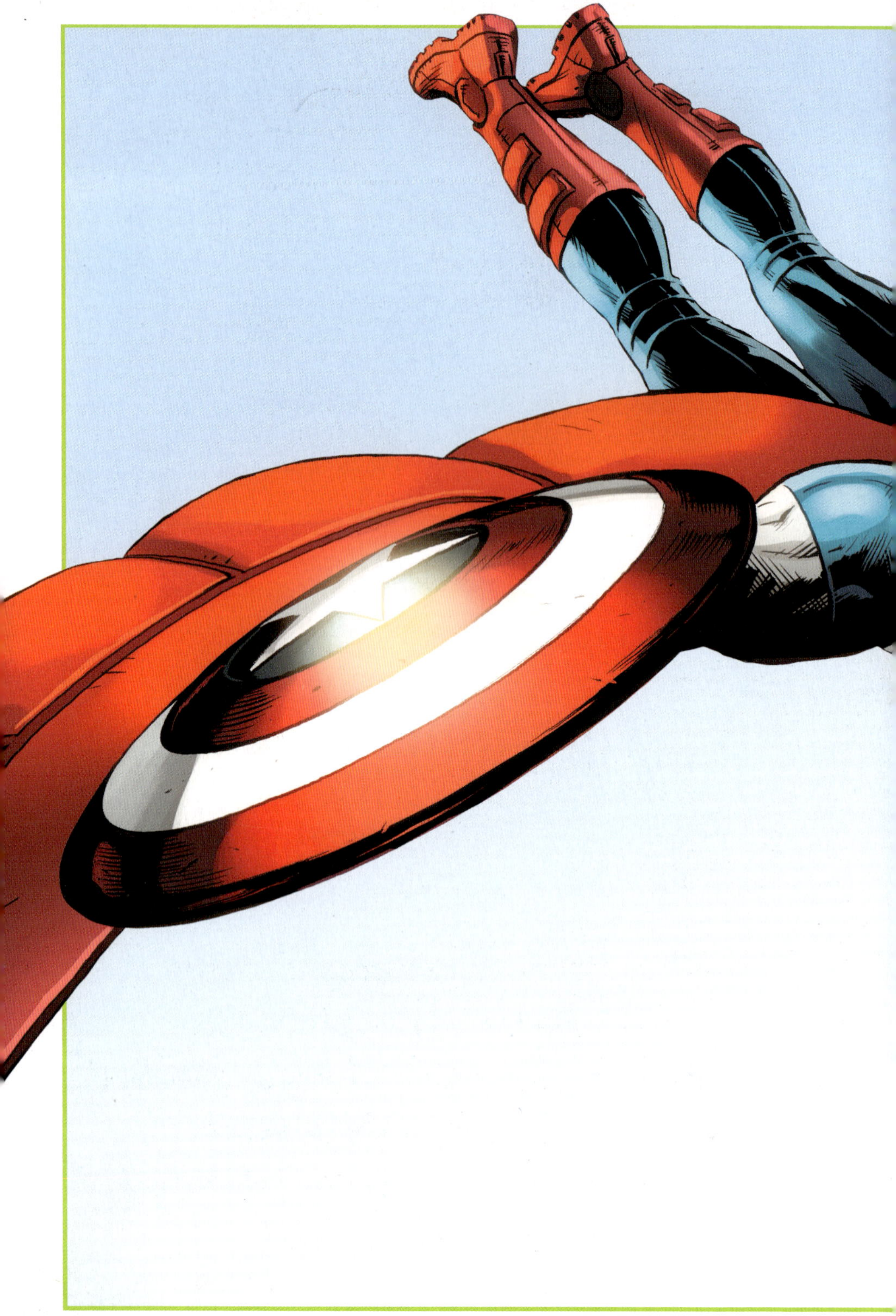

Soaring

As Captain America, Sam fights for what is right and fair. He helps people in his community and goes on missions to defeat villains. With Redwing by his side, Sam soars across the skies! He proves day after day that he is worthy of his shield.

Glossary

Champion
someone who is a winner

College
a school for older students and adults

Criminal
a person who breaks the law

Indestructible
not able to be destroyed

Inspire
to cause someone to do something great

Martial artist
someone who is a skilled fighter

Pastor
the leader of a church

Soar
to fly high in the sky

Telepathic
able to read the mind of a person or animal

Worthy
to be deserving of something

Index

Avengers 24

Birds 6, 26–27

College 22

Cosmic Cube 40

Falcon (type of bird) 28

Falcon (hero) 14

Gideon Wilson 18, 20

Goggles 9

Harlem 18

Hydra 32, 42

Iron Man 24

Martial artist 30

Misty Knight 38

Pigeons 18

Red Skull 40

Redwing 28, 42, 45

Sarah Wilson 18, 20–21

Shield 8, 9, 16, 30, 34

Spider-Man 24

Steve Rogers 10, 12, 14, 16, 34

Super Hero suit 9

Wings 6, 8, 43

Quiz

Now you have read the book, can you answer these questions?

1. What is the name of Sam's pet falcon?
2. In what city did Sam grow up?
3. Who was the first Captain America?
4. Sam led a team of mighty Super Heroes known by what name?
5. One of Sam's super-powers is that he sees what birds see. True or False?
6. What is the name of Sam's enemy who uses a Cosmic Cube to play mind tricks?
7. Which one of Sam's friends has a robotic arm?

1. Redwing 2. Harlem, New York 3. Steve Rogers 4. The Avengers 5. True 6. Red Skull 7. Misty Knight